EVERYTHINGS TURNING INTO BEAUTIFUL

A play with music

by

Seth Zvi Rosenfeld

Songs by
Jimmie James

FOUNDED 1830

New York Hollywood London Toronto
SAMUELFRENCH.COM

ISBN 978-0-573-65108-3   Printed in U.S.A.   #7138

IMPORTANT BILLING AND CREDIT REQUIREMENTS

All producers of *EVERYTHINGS TURNING INTO BEAUTI-FUL* *must* give credit to the Author of the Play in all programs distributed in connection with performances of the Play, and in all instances in which the title of the Play appears for the purposes of advertising, publicizing or otherwise exploiting the Play and /or a production. The name of the Author *must* appear on a separate line on which no other name appears, immediately following the title and *must* appear in size of type not less than fifty percent of the size of the title type.

In addition, the following credit *must* appear in all programs distributed in connection with the Work:

EVERTHING'S TURNING INTO BEAUTIFUL
A Play with Music
by Seth Zvi Rosenfeld   Songs by Jimmie James
Originally produced in New York City by the New Group
Scott Elliot, Artistic Director

THE NEW GROUP PRESENTS

EVERYTHINGS TURNING INTO *Beautiful*

a play with music

By **Seth Zvi Rosenfeld**   Songs by **Jimmie James**
Directed By **Carl Forsman**

Cast

Brenda	**Daphne Rubin-Vega**
Sam	**Malik Yoba**

sets	Beowulf Boritt
costumes	Theresa Squire
lights	Josh Bradford
sound	Daniel Baker

artistic director	Scott Elliott
executive producer	Geoff Rich
production supervisor	Peter R. Feuchtwanger/PRF Productions
production stage manager	Erin Grenier
props supervisor	Jay Duckworth
casting	Judy Henderson, C.S.A.
public relations	The Karpel Group, Bridget Klapinski

managing director, development	Oliver Dow
associate producer	Jill Bowman
associate artistic director	Ian Morgan
general manager	Amanda Brandes
marketing director	Wren Longno
company manager	Ted Hall

CHARACTERS

Brenda - *early forties*
Sam - *early forties*

Act I

(The one bedroom apartment of BRENDA. She drinks a glass of wine by herself and knits. Her doorbell rings.)

BRENDA. Who is it?
SAM. Me.
BRENDA. Sam?
SAM. Yeah.
BRENDA. Oh...

(BRENDA doesn't move. Leaves SAM at the door.)

SAM. You gonna let me in?...Bad time?
BRENDA. hhh.

(BRENDA opens the door.)

SAM. *(Whispers.)* Somebody here?
BRENDA. You know what time it is?
SAM. I saw the light on. I took a chance...Am I interrupting?
BRENDA. What are you doing here?

7

SAM. You don't know...I mean, you have no idea what I've been through...

BRENDA. Are you okay?

SAM. Is it o.k. if I come in for a minute?

SAM. I walked from Washington Heights. It's definitely not what it used to be. I miss the days when New York was scary...Fuckin' white people from Kansas meandering across a hundred forty fifth street.

BRENDA. So you walked to twenty third street?

SAM. I wrote this song!

BRENDA. You couldn't take a cab?

SAM. I didn't wanna take a cab...

BRENDA. So you walked down here at 2:00 am because you wrote a song?

(SAM sits on his couch and opens his knapsack. He digs through mountains of scrap papers, bar napkins and legal pads looking for his song.)

SAM. Yeah. You see your Knicks?

BRENDA. No.

SAM. They lost.

BRENDA. They suck.

SAM. You still have those tickets?

BRENDA. What tickets?

SAM. From those NBA people.

BRENDA. Yes.

SAM. Cause you said you'd take me, remember?

BRENDA. I haven't used them.

SAM. Cool. You wanna give me a beat?

BRENDA. What kind of beat?

SAM. Simple...Like a lunchroom beat..

BRENDA. It's hip-hop?

SAM. No...Kind of...Not really.

BRENDA. You couldn't just program that beat?

SAM. It's organic.

BRENDA. What's organic?

SAM. The song's organic. I'm not gonna fuck everything up by programming a beat.

BRENDA. By the way, Merry Christmas.

SAM. Yeah, Merry Christmas.

BRENDA. It's not a Christmas song, is it?

SAM. No...I think it's a single. I don't have a hook. You're way better with the hooks. Speaking of which, weren't we supposed to be going to St. Bart's for the holidays?

BRENDA. Right.

SAM. Remember you said...Cecil invited you and you were gonna take me.

BRENDA. I wound up not going to St. Barts.

SAM. Obviously, I never understood that. We were supposed to be on a yacht or some shit.

BRENDA. I wasn't up to it. I didn't want to sit on Cecil's yacht and pretend.

SAM. Pretend what?

BRENDA. Pretend anything. Pretend I was happy or happening or anything.

SAM. You are the happening, baby. The happening!

BRENDA. Whatever.

SAM. You know what's not happening?

BRENDA. What?

SAM. Family Court. You ever been to family court?

BRENDA. No.

SAM. It's a pit of utter fucking despair. I wish I had a camera I'd fuckin', I don't know what I'd do. I'd like to photograph — people should fuckin' see, they should see how they talk to you. It's not criminal court. Nobody's there because they committed a crime. People are there because they can't provide for their kids, ya know?...Then you have to explain to the kids. You have to say "Baby, daddy fucked over his money. Daddy wasn't thinking about you, Daddy wasn't conscious, daddy thought his hot streak was gonna last or should I say Daddy thought his luke warm streak was gonna last." Then your kid who adores you says, "It's okay daddy. I understand." You just added more drama to her mixed up little life. Then you go home and you're in a rage so you don't sleep. The voices start attacking. "You're a deadbeat dad and your kids are suffering." "You're over, finished, worthless, Mrs. Brodsky said it best in the second grade 'He's got all this potential and doesn't want to succeed'"...So I start walking from a hundred- what- eighty first street and I'm talking to God "Well if I've arrived at this", I told God, "if this is the best I can do, if I really am good for fucking nothing then let me get hit by a stray bullet. Let some random fuckin' drunk driver take me out on the way down here because I'm too fuckin' chicken to take myself." That's why I walked from Washington Heights.

BRENDA. Let me take your jacket. Did you see your kids today?

SAM. My daughter was with her Mom's family and my son is with my ex-wife.

BRENDA. You sad about that?

SAM. No, I'm not sad about that.

BRENDA. You seem sad.

SAM. You seem sad.

BRENDA. You seem sadder.

SAM. You seem saddest.

BRENDA. You seem like the ultimate sad man.

SAM. I'm not the one knitting...,What are these, socks?

BRENDA. Leg warmers.

SAM. Leg warmers? What are you, doing a revival of Flashdance?

BRENDA. Funny...Are we gonna do this song.

SAM. Alright...It's called "Naive".

BRENDA. Naive?

SAM. Right and it doesn't have a hook yet. And I need naïve in the hook.

BRENDA. Okay.

SAM. *(He goes into song. she plays a beat. he picks up an acoustic guitar and strums.)*
SPENDING TIME WITH HASTE,
SHE BEGS TO BE RESOLVED,
SHE'S FINDING ALL HER LOSS,
A SYMPTOM OF HER ILL,
I GENTLY RECOMMEND A SILENCE TO HER PLEA.
(He talks.)
This is where I need a hook.

BRENDA.
(She sings.)
SHE BOWS HER HEAD SO HUMBLE...AND NAIVE.

SAM. How'd you do that?

BRENDA. Sing...

SAM.

(Sings)
SHE'S HELD HER DISTANCE TO THE FUTURE,
A VOID TO HER PAST,
THE PRESENT IS STABLE TO HER MASKS,
I WHISPER SOMETHING TIMELY AS SHE,
CRAWLS UPON HER KNEES.

(Sam looks over at Brenda.)

    BRENDA. She turns and smiles weakly...and naive.
    SAM. How do you do that?
    BRENDA. I'm a genius.

    SAM. Here's the bridge.
(Sings.)
WE'VE BOTH BEEN BEATEN BLINDLY,
BY THE ELEMENTS OF LOVE,
WE BOTH HAVE FOUND THE EYE OF THE STORM,
THE SPACE IS ONLY BIG ENOUGH,
FOR ONE TO RESIDE,
COME TOGETHER NOT DIVIDE

    SAM. This part don't take the wrong way.
(Sings)
SHE SWALLOWS ALL SHE CAN.

    BRENDA. She swallows all she can?
    SAM. Listen.
(Sings)
AND ATTEMPTS TO GIVE AWAY,
I FIND MY LAST FEARS HAVE COME TO BEAR,

OUR EMBRACEMENT REMAINS STOLEN,
LIKE THE BEAUTY OF A SEED.

BRENDA. She moans and cries so sweetly...and naive,
I sigh and die completely...naive. *(SAM claps for her. She claps for him.)* Wow.

SAM. Yeah?

BRENDA. Yeah.

SAM. Yeah...Are you sure?

BRENDA. Yeah.

SAM. Yeah...So what do you mean by wow?

BRENDA. It's very serious.

SAM. You think?

BRENDA. Tortured.

SAM. You hate it.

BRENDA. "We've both been beaten blindly by the elements of love..." You must be tortured, Sam. You are a very tortured artist.

SAM. Okay Brenda B., do you think we can include the song.

BRENDA. I really like it a lot...Gotta go to bed. You gotta go. We have to work on the hook.

SAM. Okay, well remember before what I was saying about figuring things out.

BRENDA. You didn't say anything about figuring anything out.

SAM. I'm saying it now, Brenda.

BRENDA. Is this gonna take a long time?

SAM. No.

BRENDA. What about it?

SAM. I was thinking on the way down here that like the

process of figuring anything out, if you reduce that process, boil it down, it's really about minimizing your fear of whatever issue it is that you're pondering and if you boil that down, it's really your fear about uhh, whatever feelings might come up if you don't figure correctly. Like take me coming down here. It's a calculated risk. You may not have been home. You may be home and be with a dude. You may be home and not want to see me, right. All of these are things for me to be afraid of. They're reasons for me not to come here because all those things will make me feel sad. See, so what I'm really afraid of is feeling sad but if I go to a sad movie and I cry, it's not so bad feeling sad, it actually feels good sometimes to feel sad so maybe feeling sad isn't anything to be afraid of at all. Which is what I figured out on the walk down here. I figured the worst that could happen is you'd be with a guy cause that might be embarrassing to try and explain to him why I'd be showing up at your door at odd hours. You could tell him that we vibe together but he might not believe that...You got someone here?

BRENDA. Boundaries.

SAM. No, I know, I'm just saying.

BRENDA. I know you know.

SAM. I remember the agreement but I don't remember why we made one.

BRENDA. We discussed this when we met for lunch that first time, remember?

SAM. We did?

BRENDA. How did we meet, Sam...Remember that?

SAM. At the Mercury Lounge?

BRENDA. Right...You'd left your second wife and you were drunk and you hit on me.

SAM. Don't flatter yourself.

EVERYTHINGS TURNING INTO BEAUTIFUL

BRENDA. You didn't hit on me?

SAM. I asked you to lunch to discuss your work.

BRENDA. Right...And then what?

SAM. You laid down the law.

BRENDA. What was that law?

SAM. If we are to work together there can be no romantic anything.

BRENDA. And why Sam?

SAM. *(Imitates BRENDA.)* So we could have a safe working environment.

BRENDA. Exactly!

SAM. Let's finish...Then we discussed what?

BRENDA. I don't remember.

SAM. Attraction! That we were attracted to each other.

BRENDA. And?

SAM. And we both admitted it...That we were attracted to each other.

BRENDA. Big fucking deal. We got that out of the way and moved on.

SAM. Are you seeing somebody right now?

BRENDA. I'm not having this discussion with you.

SAM. I'd just heard all these rumors and stuff and I wanted to know, you know...what was true.

BRENDA. Which ones did you hear?

SAM. You were seeing that expressionist, graffiti artist, what's his name Guiseppi.

BRENDA. Guapo.

SAM. Guapo?...Wow...Guapo?...Guapo.

BRENDA. Stop it, Sam!

SAM. Es muy Guapo...

BRENDA. Anyway.

SAM. Then there's the one about Moses and then somebody told me you were seeing Nick.

BRENDA. People have a lot of time on their hands. I stay home. I knit. I haven't even been going out.

SAM. Why?

BRENDA. I haven't been feeling well.

SAM. What's wrong?

BRENDA. It's no big deal.

SAM. What happened?

BRENDA. I don't really wanna go into it.

SAM. Okay...Hey, life is a test.

BRENDA. Wow.

SAM. Profound, right? My stomach is really like...queasy. You don't have any chamomile tea, do you?

BRENDA. Sam!

SAM. I'll make it myself. Just tell me where the tea bags are.

BRENDA. I'm not talking about the tea.

SAM. I'll leave right after, I promise. I brought you Jimmy's CD.

(SAM ENTERS the kitchen and boils water.)

BRENDA. I got the e-mail about his show.

SAM. *(Listens for the other room.)* I just thought I heard something.

BRENDA. Don't worry about what you hear.

SAM. You should check on him. I don't wanna wake him.

BRENDA. It's a little late for that, don't you think?

SAM. A little late for who?

BRENDA. What were we talking about?

SAM. The men that you're rumored to be dating.

BRENDA. Oh, I took Moses out for dinner for his birthday that's when those rumors started. He's always so respectful. Like he's never even come on to me, ya know.

(SAM ENTERS with his tea.)

SAM. Jimmy's show was great, by the way.

BRENDA. It was Moses that invited me to St. Bart's not Cecil.

SAM. I want to put one of his songs on the album.

BRENDA. That's the reason I didn't go and that's why I couldn't invite you.

SAM. Why? I mean I thought he never came on to you.

BRENDA. I would've been his guest and wouldn't have been appropriate.

SAM. Can we just do this one song that Jimmy wrote?

BRENDA. Okay.

SAM. I want you to sing it with me.

BRENDA. I've never even heard it.

SAM. You'll get it.

(SAM slips the CD in. Hums to her...)

SAM.
YOU WERE MAD TO LET ME KNOW
I CAN'T FEEL YOU BABY SINCE I LET YOU GO
I DON'T HAVE TO UNDERSTAND

BYE BYE I UNDERSTAND
SITTIN UP CLOSE TO THE MIDDLE OF THE MOON

I CAN SEE YOU ANY NIGHT OF JUNE

   CHORUS.
MEET ME ANY NIGHT OF JUNE
MEET ME ANY NIGHT OF JUNE
MEET ME ANY NIGHT OF JUNE

*(SAM hands BRENDA the lyrics. She takes a look at them and
   then sings.)*

   BRENDA.
DON'T ASK ME WHAT TO SAY
ITS LIKE WE'RE MEETING ON A SECOND DATE
YOU MADE ME FEEL LIKE I WENT AWAY

I DON'T WANT TO GO
BUT I SHOULD HAVE NEVER LET YOU KNOW
YOU'RE THE ONE BY THE MIDDLE OF THE MOON
I'LL BE WAITING FOR YOU ANY NIGHT OF JUNE

*(They improvise a chorus together and then do a silly dance
   from the 70's a la the 4 tops. They laugh together.)*

   BRENDA. You hear my voice crack?
   SAM. Yeah.
   BRENDA. Like a boy reaching puberty or something.
   SAM. You like it?
   BRENDA. I do.
   SAM. You like me?
   BRENDA. Anyway... You think Jimmy'll let us record it.
   SAM. I'll ask him. It was sweet, wasn't it?

BRENDA. Did you see the new painting on my wall?

SAM. It's beautiful.

BRENDA. Guapo painted it.

SAM. Yeah...Muhfuckin' Guapo huh?

BRENDA. For me. He gave it to me.

SAM. Wow.

BRENDA. He had it delivered here. I opened it up and I started crying. I called him and said that I could never...but he insisted.

SAM. It's a beautiful painting.

BRENDA. I'm not seeing him. He's married.

SAM. I see.

BRENDA. We're friends, Sam.

SAM. Well maybe Guapo thinks it's more than that.

BRENDA. Why?

SAM. I don't know...Maybe you lead him on.

BRENDA. Why would you say something like that?

SAM. Maybe you're a subject of rumors because you like the attention.

BRENDA. I don't think so.

SAM. I like attention too.

BRENDA. You love attention. You live for it.

SAM. From what I can see you get a lot of guys strung out on you.

BRENDA. I do not.

SAM. But for some reason you're alone. You have no kids, no man.

BRENDA. What about you?

SAM. I have kids.

BRENDA. Three by three different women?

SAM. Two.

BRENDA. That you know about...Probably have three more from tours around the globe.

SAM. At least I'm not scared of commitment.

BRENDA. Who says you're not?

SAM. I'm here.

BRENDA. What is that supposed to mean?

SAM. Are you ever curious about me?

BRENDA. You must be really lonely this Christmas.

SAM. *(Stung.)* I'm gonna go.

BRENDA. Sam.

SAM. I'll call you after the Universal meeting.

BRENDA. Finish your tea.

SAM. I'm gonna go.

BRENDA. I am curious about you. I am curious. Especially when you're like this.

SAM. Like what?

BRENDA. I'm getting shy.

SAM. Like what?

BRENDA. Don't look at me, okay.

SAM. Okay...Can I hug you?

BRENDA. No. I'll fuckin' scream. Just talk to me.

SAM. Okay...Have you been writing?

BRENDA. I've been knitting.

SAM. You haven't written at all?

BRENDA. One thing.

SAM. Do you want to play it?

BRENDA. I want you to go.

SAM. I want to figure out what we're doing first.

BRENDA. With the CD?

SAM. With the CD...And with each other.

BRENDA. Can we do "everything's turning"?

SAM. The remix?

BRENDA. No!

SAM. The original is garbage. I like the remix.

BRENDA. It is not, baby.

SAM. You don't think so?

BRENDA. Not when you sing it honestly. The way we wrote it.

SAM. I like the remix so much better.

BRENDA. That's because you never gave this one a chance...Please.

SAM. Okay.

BRENDA. Be serious, okay? If you fuck around I'll never sing it again. I swear.

SAM. Okay...

(SAM picks up the guitar. He starts singing.)

SAM.
I SIT ALONE WITH ALL MY CRIMES,
I WASH MYSELF WITH NEW BORN EYES,
I DON'T RELY ON MY PAST SUPPLY.

HER DANCE IS TIME WITH LIGHTS THROWN ON,
SHE BRINGS ME FLOWERS IN EVERY DAWN...

BRENDA. Hold up, man.

SAM. What?

BRENDA. Did you believe yourself?

SAM. When?

BRENDA. Just now.

SAM. Yeah.

BRENDA. I didn't believe you.

SAM. What?

BRENDA. Singing that. I didn't believe you.

SAM. What are you talking about?

BRENDA. You were in your head or something.

SAM. If you say so.

BRENDA. You felt like you were authentic?

SAM. I mean, I don't know.

BRENDA. Okay, this is a problem for me.

SAM. What?

BRENDA. If you don't know when you're being truthful than everything you say is a lie.

SAM. That makes me consistent.

BRENDA. You're not gonna defend that?

SAM. I just did.

BRENDA. I can't believe this. I never thought of you as a liar, Sam. Now I definitely have questions.

SAM. Okay, what the fuck are you talking about?

BRENDA. I definitely believe that lots of times when you sing it's not from your heart.

SAM. When did this start?

BRENDA. I've had these questions for a while.

SAM. Really, well why did you agree to this partnership then?

BRENDA. It's not like I think you're untalented. When your truthful, you're amazing. You just don't know the difference between truth and untruth.

SAM. Okay, am I being truthful now?

BRENDA. Are you? You should know, Sam.

SAM. I think I am.

BRENDA. Only liars have to think about stuff like that.

SAM. And you're always truthful?

BRENDA. Yes.

SAM. You're fulla shit. You lie all the time.

BRENDA. Name one time.

SAM. Is there somebody in the other room?

BRENDA. I'm not answering that. Weren't you going to go?

SAM. Who are you seeing?

BRENDA. I'm not getting into that with you.

SAM. Who would be acceptable for you?

BRENDA. Someone nice. Someone kind. Someone who doesn't show up at your door at odd hours.

SAM. I don't believe you.

BRENDA. No?

SAM. I think you have so many rules that you keep yourself all alone.

BRENDA. If you say so. We've both said a lot tonight. Why don't we sleep on it?

SAM. Is there somebody in the other room?

BRENDA. Why are you paranoid?

SAM. Is someone in there?

BRENDA. Sam, I'm having a hard time getting through Christmas. I'm tired. I'm PMS-ing. Is any of this landing on you?

SAM. It is.

BRENDA. I have to go to LA in two weeks and do a jingle for some shitty TV show just to make ends meet.

SAM. That is so beautiful.

BRENDA. What is so beautiful?

SAM. You're still at it. Still fighting. Still creating.

BRENDA. Oh my God. Who are you?

SAM. I really do think you're beautiful.
BRENDA. Look at my body.
SAM. I like your body.
BRENDA. You date twenty six year olds.
SAM. So do you.
BRENDA. I don't have a twenty six year old body.

(BRENDA laughs.)

SAM. I don't have a twenty six year old body either.
BRENDA. I know.
SAM. Don't say it like that!
BRENDA. I like your body.
SAM. You do.
BRENDA. You're sexy.
SAM. Stop.
BRENDA. Look at you, all shy. What happened to Mr. Tough guy?
SAM. I'm not shy.
BRENDA. You seem shy.
SAM. You win the Grammy for shy.
BRENDA. You win the Presidential academy award for shy.
SAM. That was corny.
BRENDA. Come sit with me.

(SAM sits on the couch next to BRENDA.)

BRENDA. You know you're sexy, right? I've been watching you for a while.
SAM. Oh yeah.

BRENDA. So umm, what, you wanna fuck?

SAM. What?

BRENDA. That's why you came here, right? It's Christmas, I mean, you're a guy, I'm a girl, we're both grown, right?

(BRENDA strokes his chest. BRENDA goes to kiss him. He pulls away.)

SAM. What are you doing?

BRENDA. Just what I thought!

SAM. What?

BRENDA. You can't take it.

SAM. Can't take what?

BRENDA. You really can't take it.

SAM. What are you talking about?

BRENDA. You chase, chase, chase —

SAM. Hold on a minute.

BRENDA. What happened with Shoshanna?

SAM. What happened with Shoshanna?

BRENDA. She's my friend, Sam!

SAM. So?

BRENDA. So she told me —

SAM. — About what? Nothing ever happened.

BRENDA. That's exactly what she said.

SAM. What are you talking about?

BRENDA. Why Sam? Why didn't anything happen?

SAM. Because I didn't like her.

BRENDA. When did you figure that out?

SAM. What do you mean?

BRENDA. When did you figure out that you didn't like her?

SAM. I don't know...She's not really a nice person.

BRENDA. What's not nice about her?

SAM. She's withholding. I don't like how she treats her kid.

BRENDA. When did you figure this out? It wasn't when you were chasing after her. It was after she relented.

SAM. Relented?

BRENDA. After you fucked her.

SAM. This has nothing to do with her.

BRENDA. You don't get it.

SAM. You don't get it. You think you can know me by gathering information and gossip and all this other shit from other people?

BRENDA. Some things.

SAM. No, you think if you gather enough information you can protect yourself.

BRENDA. I think information is part of knowing someone, Sam.

SAM. So you think people can't change?

BRENDA. I think people have patterns.

SAM. And change is impossible?

BRENDA. Change is hard.

SAM. You have any idea what I've been through?!

BRENDA. I know what you've been through.

SAM. You don't have a fucking clue. Your friends can't tell you what's beating in my chest for you, Brenda...When you look in my eyes what do you see?

BRENDA. I'm not playing this game.

SAM. When you look in my eyes what do you see?

BRENDA. Sam —

SAM. Look.

(BRENDA stares into SAM'S eyes.)

BRENDA. I see a gentle soul. I see an Eagle. I see lost time.

SAM. You want to know what I see when I look in your eyes?

BRENDA. No.

SAM. Okay.

(SAM picks up a guitar and starts to play.)

BRENDA. Alright.

SAM. What?

BRENDA. When you look in my eyes what do you see?

SAM. Fear. Mystery...Yearning.

BRENDA. Next you'll tell about my fear of intimacy, how my inappropriate relationship with my father scarred me for life. Not to mention the rape in Italy when I was eighteen. I've had twelve years of therapy, you can't cure me.

SAM. I don't want to cure you.

BRENDA. You don't? I've watched you, Sam.

SAM. What do you see?

BRENDA. Your wife.

SAM. Which one?

BRENDA. You find these little birds with broken wings who fell for you because you promised to fix them but you didn't fix them, you broke them worse. Like the worst kind of predator, Sam. You don't come with a bottle of Cristal you seduce with a cure and the moment you realize that you've got no cure, that we're all different versions of the same hopeless case, you bounce. The relationship is over and you can have some fancy diagnosis of why. Some shit that you tell yourself so you can sleep at night...She's withholding...You're a dangerous man with that shit

(Beat.)

SAM. You really don't like me.
BRENDA. I didn't say that.
SAM. It's obvious.
BRENDA. I don't like some things about you.
SAM. I don't like some things about me either.
BRENDA. I like you when you're funny.
SAM. I'm not always gonna be a fuckin' barrel of laughs, Brenda...
BRENDA. I know that...Let's do Seu Todo Bom.
SAM. I don't wanna do the MC HAMMER song.
BRENDA. It's not MC HAMMER. It's fun. It's a single. We get Pharell to do a remix. Snoop or somebody could do the intro.

(BRENDA opens up her closet. She takes out a pimp hat and hands it to SAM. She puts on a fur coat. Pulls up her pajama bottoms and makes them look like hot pants. Then puts on some high heels.)

SAM. You are killing me right now.
BRENDA. Let's do the video...Okay...Take the camera and we film each other...
SAM. Are you serious?

(BRENDA starts filming SAM it's projected onto a large screen behind them.)

SAM. Don't show it to anybody.

(BRENDA puts in the CD SAM starts miming doing his part in the video. It's upbeat. Danceable and SAM is doing his performance. BRENDA dressed like a hooker does a stripper dance. SAMS takes the camera and films her.)

WHEN YOU DANCE
YOU SEND ME A THRILL
WHEN YOU SMILE
YOU SEND ME A THRILL

WHEN WE MAKE LOVE
SEU TODA BOM

WHEN WE KISS
YOU SEND ME A THRILL
WHEN WE TOUCH
YOU GIVE ME A CHILL

WHEN WE MAKE LOVE
SU TODO BUENO

WHEN YOU DANCE
YOU SEND ME A THRILL
WHEN YOU SMILE
YOU SEND ME A THRILL

WHEN WE MAKE LOVE
SUO TUTTO BUONO

ITS ALL GOOD
SEU TODO BOM
IT'S ALL GOOD
SU TODO BUENO
IT'S ALL GOOD
SON TOUT BON
IT'S ALL GOOD
SUO TUTTO BUONO
REAL...

SAM. Was I lying then?
BRENDA. Were you?
SAM. You seem to be the expert on me.
BRENDA. I believed you that time.
SAM. Yeah?
BRENDA. Do you think we can sell records?
SAM. I do.
BRENDA. The way the industry is?
SAM. I don't look at it like that.
BRENDA. Like what?
SAM. I don't see the lack.
BRENDA. What do you see?
SAM. I see the possibility.
BRENDA. You're a dreamer.
SAM. Maybe I am.
BRENDA. You're not based in reality.
SAM. Maybe not.
BRENDA. That's a problem for me. I'm trying to have a real life.
SAM. Other night, I gigged for the fun of it at "The Living Room".

BRENDA. You didn't call me.

SAM. It was spur of the moment...Jimmy and Gerald came through and we jammed and whatever,...I'm done...I'm bullshitting with some people..It's late...This cat gets up with his guitar and his harp and it's eight people in the room and not one of them is here to see him...He's not young, he's not old, to tell you the truth I couldn't tell you one thing about how the cat loooked but he strapped on his harmonica and started doin' it, man...He was screamin' it...screamin' through his harp "Listen up, baby, I'm here to play!"...Screaming the shit, Brenda, turning the shit out...We all stopped what we were doing and paid close attention...They passed around the hat...He took his twenty dollars and was in the wind...I can't remember his name but the motherfucker put a smile on my face...Got me through the next day. Probably got him through too...That was real to me.

BRENDA. Is that really enough to get you through the day?

SAM. Yes.

BRENDA. For me it's not. For me I want things. Big things. I want all the things. I want the cake and to eat it too and not get fat. Can you make that happen?

SAM. Well what are big things?

BRENDA. I want money...A lot of it...I don't want to have to work that hard to get it...I want to make a CD...Play some dates...Sell a lot of records...And then take the money...Run off with my man to a small town in Provence...Live in one of those old stone houses and make a baby...Make music...Hibernate... Come back after a while and people are watering at the mouth for my next album and then I do it, make a few more million... Write children's books....

SAM. Don't say study the Kaballah.

BRENDA. Not like that! I've always wanted to write childrens books...Actually I've written

Children's books but I've never shown anyone.

SAM. Can I —

BRENDA. No, I'm not finished...I want two more kids.... Maybe adopted...I want a husband who's not a drug addict, who's capable of being intimate and loving and kind and faithful...Not like a musician...What else...I want to have fun...I want to play...I want to play in the water and dance...I want to rollerskate...I want to live in Mallorca...I want to live in Spain and I want to learn to dance the Flamenca...I want to buy a loft... Not here...Not in Chelsea...In umm....Chinatown...I want to eat Chinese food at five AM and never gain any weight and not have to go the Gym...I want to be like those Island women with perfect posture who have beautiful bodies til they're eighty...

SAM. Sounds tremendous.

BRENDA. Tremendous?

SAM. Yeah.

BRENDA. Is that all you have to say?

SAM. No, I mean, I want you to have all those things.

BRENDA. What about you?

SAM. I don't know...I want you...I know that.

BRENDA. I can't even have a conversation with you.

SAM. We don't have to talk.

BRENDA. Yeah whatever...Do you realize we don't have any political songs?

SAM. Do you want to write something political?

BRENDA. I want us to care.

SAM. Who says we don't care?

BRENDA. I want us to really care, Sam!

SAM. Okay... Do you want to play the song that you've been writing?

BRENDA. No!...You're not listening.

SAM. I mean like, I agree with you. I hear what you're saying.

BRENDA. We're very different. We don't like the same things. We don't want the same things.

SAM. Is that why you aren't my girlfriend?

BRENDA. I'm too old to be somebody's "girlfriend". That would make you my "Boyfriend" and I'm actually in the market for a "Man"...Maybe you're not quite sure what that is yet.

SAM. I'll drag you by your hair into the fucking bedroom.

BRENDA. I dare you.

SAM. You dare me?

(In one motion SAM scoops BRENDA up into his arms.)

BRENDA. I'm joking...I'm joking...You're a big, strong monster of a man. Please put me down...*(SAM puts BRENDA down.)* Do you have a hard on, right now?

SAM. No.

BRENDA. You caught a little wood, baby? I thought I felt something poking me.

SAM. It was my belt buckle.

BRENDA. You're not wearing a belt.

SAM. I'm in love with you.

BRENDA. You're not saying you're in love with me Sam. You have to be more responsible than to just spit shit out like that.

SAM. I love you.

BRENDA. We're supposed to go into the studio next week.

SAM. I know.

BRENDA. I don't want to ruin something that's great.

SAM. It won't.

BRENDA. I've got somebody inside.

SAM. Who?

BRENDA. Doesn't matter.

SAM. You're lying.

BRENDA. I'm not.

SAM. Yeah, you are. I know you. You're lying.

BRENDA. You don't know that. You don't know what I do late at night. I mean, nobody told you to come here so late.

(SAM kisses her. They kiss long and passionate. She pushes him off of her.)

BRENDA. You ruined a great partnership, Sam...A great partnership...

SAM. Brenda —

BRENDA. We had a great partnership and now it's ruined forever!

SAM. Forever-ever?

BRENDA. I'm being serious. Don't make fun of me when I'm being serious. We had a great partnership and now it's ruined.

SAM. You wanna play a song?

BRENDA. No!

SAM. Just to see if we can still play together after we kissed.

BRENDA. I am exhausted!

SAM. One last song will determine our fate. If not I'll go.

BRENDA. I'm not picking...you pick.

SAM. Stealing a soul?

BRENDA. No. We're not doing that. We're doing "Picture me"!

SAM. I thought you said I pick.

BRENDA. I changed my mind.

SAM. Really?

BRENDA. I guess you're the only one allowed to do that.

SAM. Who starts?

BRENDA. Just play.

(Beat...BRENDA picks up the guitar...She plays with conviction... Stares at SAM and softens..)

BRENDA.
PICTURE ME IN YOUR HEART
PICTURE ME ON YOUR SIDE
PICTURE ME IN THE BACK SEAT OF YOUR CAR

PICTURE ME IN YOUR HEAD
PICTURE ME IN YOUR BED
PICTURE ME BUYING YOU A NEW GUITAR

(He joins her.)

BOTH.
CHORUS.
LA LA LA
LA LA LA LA LA LA
LA LA LA LA LA LA

SAM.
PICTURE ME IN YOUR HEART
PICTURE ME BY YOUR SIDE
PICTURE ME IN THE BEST DAYS OF YOUR LIFE

*(Beat. SAM and BRENDA hold hands for a brief moment and
then she pulls away.)*

BRENDA. ...You hungry?

SAM. I'm starving.

BRENDA. You want me to cook something? That's what
you guys always want. You show up at two in the morning. You
wanna eat and you wanna fuck or you wanna fuck then you
wanna eat. In your case you wanna play music, have lots of
angst and eat. That's what it seems like to me —

SAM. I'm so hungry for you...

(He spins her around and kisses her again. She smiles.)

BRENDA. Say that again.

SAM. I'm so hungry for you.

BRENDA. Say you won't hurt me.

SAM. I won't hurt you.

BRENDA. ...Don't hurt me, Sam...I'll get my big brother
on you.

(He picks her up and takes her into the bedroom. Lights out.)

END OF ACT I

ACT II

(BRENDA'S bedroom. BRENDA lays on SAM'S chest. Both are
*   near naked.*
SAM may be sleeping.)

>   BRENDA. Sam?
>   SAM. Huh?
>   BRENDA. Don't sleep.
>   SAM. I'm not...

(SAM starts to snore.)

>   BRENDA. Sam!
>   SAM. I'm not sleeping...I'm cuddling...I'm cuddling.
>   BRENDA. Did you enjoy it?
>   SAM. Mmm, hmmm.
>   BRENDA. What was your favorite part?
>   SAM. Everything.

(Beat.)

>   BRENDA. Was it the best orgasm you've ever had in your
> life?

SAM. It was.
BRENDA. You roared like a lion.

(She roars like a lion.)

SAM. That was you.
BRENDA. Sam, what's your most favorite song?
SAM. Not now.
BRENDA. Hum it. Please and I'll guess the title and the band.

(SAM hums his favorite song.)

BRENDA. I need words.
SAM. How many?
BRENDA. Five crucial ones.

(SAM hums and then sings.)

SAM.
— CAN'T FIND MY WAY HOME....

BRENDA. I know that song. That was Ginger Baker, Steve Winwood and Eric Clapton.
SAM. Good.
BRENDA. Was that Cream?
SAM. No.
BRENDA. Traffic?
SAM. No.
BRENDA. I give up.
SAM. Blind Faith.

BRENDA. Blind Faith.....Sam, why do you think you never had a song like that?

SAM. What?

BRENDA. I mean, you write really wonderful songs but you've never has a big hit like that.

SAM. You're right.

BRENDA. I wonder that about myself but like I did have that one song.

SAM. Brenda.

BRENDA. It went all the way to number two and stayed most of the summer.

SAM. Come here.

BRENDA. It went platinum...You've never had that. Why? It's not for lack of talent.

SAM. There's lots of talented people.

BRENDA. We're talking about you.

SAM. The show ain't over yet.

BRENDA. I know that but til now.

SAM. I don't know.

BRENDA. I can say in retrospect that after that single people wanted different versions of that same song and I was just unwilling to play ball. I remember telling my manager that I'd never sing that song again and it was the only one the audience really wanted to hear...You've had deals everywhere. People still believe in your talent. What is it?

SAM. Why are you bringing this up now?

BRENDA. I'm curious about you!

SAM. I think I liked you better when you weren't so curious.

BRENDA. Everybody always wants something then they get it and can't handle it. Maybe that's why you've never really hit.

SAM. Maybe you're right. Maybe just when I'm about to get the things I want most I stop showing up.

BRENDA. I'm glad you said that.

SAM. Why?

BRENDA. Because I agree with that assessment.

SAM. Then it's solved.

BRENDA. So do you plan on showing up this time?

SAM. What?

BRENDA. With us.

SAM. With our CD?

BRENDA. ...Yeah.

SAM. Haven't I been showing up?

BRENDA. You have...And I really appreciate that...*(Beat.)* So tell me more about your marriages.

SAM. What do you want to know?

BRENDA. Let's say you had a new relationship. What would you do different?

SAM. What are you doing?

BRENDA. What would be different with me than with your two wives?

SAM. You're not them, first of all.

BRENDA. Yeah well, I was at Eunice's wedding and I ran into my friend Michelle.

SAM. Michelle Hughes?

BRENDA. Yeah. You know now she's living with John.

SAM. I know.

BRENDA. So I asked her like how's it going with John, ya know?...She said he's terrific, he's a hundred eighty degrees from her last boyfriend, his name was John too, right?

SAM. I remember.

BRENDA. Then she said her relationship with John is identical to the one she had with the other John because she hasn't changed a bit...So now she's on a mission to make herself better.

SAM. I see your point.

BRENDA. Your first two marriages were disasters.

SAM. Have a little discretion.

BRENDA. Those are your words.

SAM. I said disaster?

BRENDA. You said tremendous disasters. Failures on every level.

SAM. There was love there.

BRENDA. Is there still love?

SAM. I mean, once you love somebody like that. There's always love, right....You might hate them , wanna spit on them or something but...there's love.

BRENDA. Tell me a story.

SAM. A story?

BRENDA. Something you've never told anyone...Please.

SAM. Can I get fifteen minutes of uninterrupted sleep, I mean cuddling afterwards?

BRENDA. With your eyes open or closed?

SAM. Closed.

BRENDA. Okay but you can't sleep.

SAM. Okay.

BRENDA. What's the secret? Make it juicy, okay?

SAM. Okay...When I was a kid in this game and ya know I was supposed to be the next big somebody, right.

BRENDA. Yeah.

SAM. It was cool. I partied with all my heroes. Got gifts from people I didn't know. Man, they threw parties for me. I remember one time in LA A&M through a party for me at the Roxbury. Prince was there, Eddie Murphy, Wilt Chamberlain...

BRENDA. Arsenio?

SAM. Arsenio stayed home that night. I'm in the VIP and it's all these people and I don't know any of them, really. I found myself thinking about who my people are. Are my family my people? My mom, is she my people? My girl? I'm high and shit and I'm thinkin' who are my people...Who are my people?... These people look good...They keep telling me how talented I am. They must be my people...Am I my people?...Am I my people?...Cause I got this hole inside of me that I wake up with every morning and if these people find out...How broken I really am... And that was the moment...I knew that I'd find a way to fuck this whole thing up.

BRENDA. Sam! No!

SAM. The secret part is that I just never felt like much...Ya know?....So like you ask me about my marriages and my career and the opportunities I've wasted and ummm....You know... fuck, God gives everyone a chance to be productive, he opens the fuckin doors you gotta step in and do your job and you don't get a hundred chances...Lots of times you get one great chance. One great chance. One big door opens and you either step all the way the fuck in or you lose...That door opened for me... Widely...and I wasn't wise. I wasn't productive or graceful and so it shut in front of me. That's how I look at it. So if by God's grace that it opens again Brenda. I will be the most productive. I will fulfill my God given potential. Believe that.

BRENDA. I hope it does.

SAM. Me too. That's why I don't want to fuck this up.

BRENDA. You don't want to fuck what up?

SAM. You promised fifteen minutes —

BRENDA. I want you to finish though. You don't want to fuck what up?

SAM. I just think your instincts are dead on.

BRENDA. With what?

SAM. The relationship thing.

BRENDA. What about it?

SAM. How it complicates the work and things.

BRENDA. Right...What are you saying?

SAM. Nothing...Can we just rest...Like breathe.

BRENDA. You said before that you were in love with me.

SAM. I know.

BRENDA. Has something changed?

SAM. Yes....I mean, no

BRENDA. What do you mean?

SAM. I mean no. Nothing's changed.

BRENDA. This was kind of a big deal.

SAM. I know.

BRENDA. It's been a long time for me.

SAM. It has?

BRENDA. Yes.

SAM. How long?

BRENDA. I'm embarrassed.

SAM. Let's just drop it.

BRENDA. Over a year.

SAM. Wow...What'd you, take a vow of celibacy?

BRENDA. I just closed up shop. That's it. Closed for business. Ya know?...How long for you?

SAM. I'm not telling.

BRENDA. Why?

SAM. You'll get mad.

BRENDA. We didn't make any commitments to each

other.

    SAM. I know but —

    BRENDA. Just tell me.

    SAM. Four days.

    BRENDA. Four days?

    SAM. Look at you.

    BRENDA. I'm not mad. With who?

    SAM. Doesn't matter.

    BRENDA. It doesn't?

    SAM. It was nothing.

    BRENDA. What do you mean? What was the problem?

    SAM. What do you mean?

    BRENDA. Why not have a relationship with her?

    SAM. Wouldn't work.

    BRENDA. Why?

    SAM. I don't wanna get into it.

    BRENDA. Why?

    SAM. I see where this is going and there's nothing good that's gonna come out of it.

    BRENDA. Sam!

    SAM. How 'bout that uninterrupted cuddling —

    BRENDA. It's too late for that now. Like you said the door is swung open.

    SAM. Look Brenda —

    BRENDA. No Sam, why not have a relationship with her.

    SAM. Because two minutes into the thing I saw she has major Unresolved daddy shit.

    BRENDA. Unresolved daddy shit.

    SAM. Yeah.

    BRENDA. Unresolved daddy shit...Wow...But that didn't stop you from fucking her.

SAM. Why are you so vulgar?

BRENDA. Who was she?

SAM. You don't wanna know.

BRENDA. I know the person?

SAM. Oh Jesus.

BRENDA. I know the person! Are you like seeing her?

SAM. No.

BRENDA. Then what?

SAM. It was a thing. A distraction.

BRENDA. A distraction? You're saying she was a distraction? You call a woman that you fucked a distraction and yet I'm the vulgar one.

SAM. If you knew who it was you'd understand.

BRENDA. So who was it?

SAM. I can't tell you.

BRENDA. Who was it?

SAM. You're gonna think I'm so cheap.

BRENDA. Sam, I'll hit you with an ashtray!

SAM. It was Alisa.

(Beat)

BRENDA. Please tell me you didn't.

SAM. I did.

BRENDA. Ewww. Ewww!

SAM. I know.

BRENDA. Sam! She's so gross.

SAM. It was late. We were at some stupid party.

BRENDA. I can't hear another word. I can't believe you!

SAM. They asked me to walk her home…

BRENDA. You're a fuckin' slut!

(She gets up out of bed. Throws clothes around.)

BRENDA. I have to take a shower. Oh my God, I'm so stupid...Rats! Foiled again. I can't ever make a smart move when it comes to men.

SAM. You asked me a question.

BRENDA. And you were stupid enough to answer!

SAM. What was I supposed to do?

BRENDA. Lie!

SAM. Lie?!

BRENDA. There are times when the truth is inappropriate, Sam. This would be one of them.

SAM. I can see how you might say that but —

BRENDA. There is no fucking but, Sam — There's no but. You don't tell somebody that you've just had sex with that you had sex with the biggest slut in New York City history four days ago... That's really not a good look for you, Sam.

(She takes her hand and mushes his face.)

SAM. You just mushed me!

BRENDA. Yeah I fuckin mushed you!

SAM. Wow, you mushed me, I'm gonna go.

BRENDA. Good.

(Beat. SAM gets dressed.)

SAM. I was honest with you because you're always accusing me of being a liar and the only reason I ever slept with anybody else is to take the pain away from not having you.

BRENDA. You expect me to believe that? I am not a twenty

two year old groupie, Sam.

SAM. You know who you are?

BRENDA. Who am I?

SAM. You are a miserable person.

BRENDA. Miserable?

SAM. Miserable. And you're not gonna be happy until you make both of us miserable. I'm not gonna stay here and be miserable with you.

BRENDA. You wanna know me.

SAM. No.

BRENDA. You wanna hear my new song?

SAM. No.

(SAM is finished dressing. BRENDA is near tears.)

BRENDA. ...Stay and listen to my song, Sam....I'm sorry I mushed you. Please stay and listen. It's called "A Safe Place". *(She sings directly to him from a soft spot in her heart.)*
I HAVE NO LIFE, NO FRIENDS OF MY OWN,
I HIDE WHAT I HAVE, I KEEP IT ALONE,
I KEEP WHAT I HAVE, WITH NO HELP OF MY OWN,
I DON'T WANT TO BE HERE ANYMORE...

I'M NEVER QUITE SURE IF IT'S ME OR IT'S YOU,
AND I NEVER KNOW EXACTLY WHAT IT IS I SHOULD
    DO,
I'M AFRAID THAT A CHANGE WOULD OPEN A DOOR,
I DON'T WANT TO BE HERE ANYMORE...

I LEFT MANY TIMES I WANT YOU TO KNOW,
SO DON'T BE AFRAID THAT I JUST WOULDN'T GO,

IT'S HARD TO EXPLAIN WHY I COULDN'T WANT
    MORE,
I DON'T WANT TO BE HERE ANYMORE...

IT MAY SEEM TO A FEW THAT IT'S SAD I'M ALIVE,
TO LIVE WITH SO LITTLE, TO BARELY SURVIVE,
BUT TO FIND A SAFE PLACE IS HARD TO IGNORE,
I DON'T WANT TO BE HERE ANYMORE...

TO BE ALONE I'M NEVER QUITE SURE,
WILL BE WHAT I WANT AND NOT TO WANT MORE,
I ALWAYS FORGET WHAT STARTED THE WAR,
I DON'T WANT TO BE HERE ANYMORE.

(BRENDA stops. SAM stares at her. Tears come to his eyes.)

    SAM. That song made me think about my father...Making
Pancakes.
    BRENDA. Making pancakes?
    SAM. My father used to make pancakes. I loved my
father's pancakes.
    BRENDA. Have you ever had my pancakes?
    SAM. No.
    BRENDA. I use a secret ingredient.
    SAM. What's that?
    BRENDA. Cinnamon.
    SAM. Wow, that's really secret.
    BRENDA. Shut up.
    SAM. I liked your song.
    BRENDA. You did?
    SAM. I liked it a lot.

BRENDA. I finished it today. When did you finish "Naive"?

SAM. Tonight.

BRENDA. What time?

SAM. Around midnight.

BRENDA. Mine was nine AM.

SAM. Nine am?

BRENDA. I had insomnia. What were you thinking about when you wrote "Naive".

SAM. What do you think?

BRENDA. It was about me, wasn't it?

SAM. Basically the thought that came was that love is always naive.

BRENDA. Why?

SAM. Brenda?

BRENDA. What?

SAM. A lot has happened and maybe we should talk tomorrow.

BRENDA. Don't you want to know what I was thinking about when I was writing?

SAM. What were you thinking about?

BRENDA. I was in bed...Alone and I was writing and —

(Her breathing starts to get heavy. She pauses. It's as if she's gotten dizzy.)

SAM. What's the matter?

BRENDA. Shit...I have to sit down.

(BRENDA sits.)

SAM. What's the matter?
BRENDA. Touch my heart.

(SAM puts his hand on her heart.)

BRENDA. Is it beating really fast?
SAM. No.
BRENDA. I'm having a heart attack, Sam!
SAM. I don't think so.
BRENDA. Call nine one one.
SAM. Your heart is fine.
BRENDA. I'm having problems breathing.
SAM. Let's go by the window.
BRENDA. I can't get up. Sam please. Take me to the hospital.
SAM. I'll open the window.

(SAM opens the window.)

BRENDA. I'm dying Sam. I'm dying.
SAM. You want some water?
BRENDA. Yes. Please.
SAM. Have you ever had a panic attack?
BRENDA. Yes...I'm not having one...I can't breathe.
SAM. I think you are.
BRENDA. I'm not.
SAM. I'm an expert I've had like 400 of them.
BRENDA. Stop.
SAM. And each time I think I'm having a heart attack. I start screaming, like a seventh grade girl. "Take me to the hospital, I'm having a heart attack!"

BRENDA. Don't make me laugh, Sam.

SAM. I'm serious, I've been to the hospital over twenty times for panic attacks. To this day, if I walk into St. Lukes they go "You're not having a heart attack , Sam".

(She laughs.)

SAM. I tell them you don't understand the amount of drugs and cigarettes and cholesterol. They're like, "you're fine". I demand stress tests, cardiograms, sonagrams, telegrams, teddy grahams, singing telegrams, the whole nine.

BRENDA. How'd they come out?

SAM. Good. I run six miles every other day. I go to the Gym. I'm alright....You alright?

(BRENDA can't answer.)

SAM. Talk to me...You alright?

BRENDA. People think I'm crazy.

SAM. I know. They say that about you.

BRENDA. Please don't make me laugh...Do they really say that?

SAM. They do.

BRENDA. Does that bug you?

SAM. Sometimes.

BRENDA. Do you think I'm crazy?

SAM. Do you think you are?

BRENDA. Sometimes.

SAM. In what way?

BRENDA. I'm having a panic attack talking about a song I wrote. There's insanity in my family. My mother's out of her mind, my father's completely depressed. I've been in and out of therapy for years and nothing seems to change. I've tried medication and stuff. I don't know. I mean I thought that by this time, I'd have kids and a family and I'm just so pissed that it's not in the cards for me. How'd I get here? That's what I wonder. Did I have a good time the first half of my life? I was so focused on making music and living like a rock star and the fucking scene. Then you try to back your way into some kind of normal life and nothing fits. What is it to have a family? To have kids running around. To go shopping for clothes for them and know what their favorite meals are and to be up on the new toys and cartoons and to be responsible for more than your own pathetic life. What is it to have a decent, healthy relationship that doesn't include Cops at your door and finding drugs in your bathroom and...the pain...I know so much about pain, Sam...I can't take anymore pain...I really can't. I want something decent but I have no experience of it...I really don't know what decency looks like. Is it what my parents had? I was listening to you talking about wanting to die and I wish I was passionate enough about life to want to die but it's not that for me...I have problems living. Like actually living! Feeling that anything new, anything new...I want something new to happen— — Something new — Something brand new, Sam!...Something that changes my perspective on being alive! Don't smile Sam. That's what I was thinking about when I wrote that song and you have no idea how deadly serious I am!

SAM. I want you to listen to me, okay?

BRENDA. Okay.

SAM. You ever wonder why I say to you that I can only work with you one or two days a week?

BRENDA. I know you're busy and this isn't your only

project. It's not mine either.

SAM. I have problems sleeping.

BRENDA. Me too.

SAM. After I see you. I have problems sleeping.

BRENDA. Really?

SAM. I keep thinking it's gonna go away. I keep thinking that I can think my way out of it. That I can talk myself out of it. I think of eight hundred reasons why it shouldn't work and then every time I see you...

BRENDA. Sam —

SAM. It grows.

BRENDA. They say your spirit can only grow in love so maybe it's that your spirit is growing and you're thinking that it's connected to me.

SAM. You just made no sense at all.

BRENDA. I know.

SAM. I called that song "Naive" because it's the naive part that's allowing me to fall in love with you.

(Beat. What SAM has just said has opened her eyes. BRENDA is silent. She gathers herself.)

BRENDA. I don't want a love that's naive.

SAM. I'm not saying that that's the only quality —

BRENDA. I don't want that.

SAM. What do you want?

BRENDA. I want a love that's accountable.

SAM. Right, okay, I think you're misunderstanding what I'm saying to you.

BRENDA. I don't think so. I want a love that's responsible. That pays bills and gets up in the morning.

(BRENDA stops herself from crying.)

SAM. I am responsible.

BRENDA. In what way?

SAM. I'm a good dad.

BRENDA. Is that why you're in family court?

SAM. One thing has nothing to do with the other.

BRENDA. I think it does maybe you love your kids in a way that's naive but maybe you're not responsible. Do you have College Funds for them?

SAM. What the fuck does that have to do with anything?

BRENDA. Do you?

SAM. No.

BRENDA. Do you have a Will?

SAM. No.

BRENDA. Is that responsible and accountable?

SAM. How do you feel about me having kids?

BRENDA. It's not the kids that bug me, it's the family court, the ex-wives, the payments, the chaos and the drama.

SAM. Forget the drama. How do you feel about me having kids?...Is it a plus or a minus?...Be honest.

BRENDA. It's a minus because I know you like to spend time with them and that means that you wouldn't be as focused on me.

SAM. Is there a good part of me having kids?

BRENDA. I don't wanna say.

SAM. Why?

BRENDA. Cause then you'll get your hopes up and you'll ultimately be disappointed.

SAM. You don't even need me here. You can have every conversation between you, yourself and you.

BRENDA. Okay Sam, the good part about you having kids is let's say we were together and stuff and we lived together or whatever.

SAM. Right.

BRENDA. The kids could come over on the weekend and maybe it could be like we had a real family.

SAM. Yeah.

BRENDA. That would be the really beautiful part but don't get your hopes up.

SAM. Why?

(BRENDA doesn't answer.)

SAM. What's the matter?

BRENDA. I'm not up for this. I'm really not.

SAM. You're not up for what?

BRENDA. I can't go where you want me to.

SAM. Where do you think I want you to go?

BRENDA. I don't want to have a relationship with you.

SAM. Since when?

BRENDA. Since I have my eyes wide open and I'm not willing to close them so that you'll fit because I could love you.

SAM. What do you see that makes it so hard to imagine yourself with me?

BRENDA. You really want to do this?

SAM. Do what?

BRENDA. Make this unpleasant.

SAM. Unpleasant? Do you think this has been like a fuckin stroll in the park so far?...Let's just get it all out.

BRENDA. Sam, I see someone who's love has got to be

naive because he's got to trick himself into falling and doesn't have the stamina and the maturity to stick it out.

SAM. That's funny, because I look at you and I see someone who invents reasons to stay all alone.

BRENDA. I see someone who thinks he can analyze other people but really doesn't even know himself.

SAM. Because I haven't had 12 years of therapy?

BRENDA. Because mostly everything you say is fantasy based, Sam.

SAM. How the fuck would you know? Are you supposed to be the grounded one? You're not the gold standard for sanity.

BRENDA. I know because I pay close attention and I see a man who at his center doesn't love himself!

SAM. Wait a minute.

BRENDA. And what could a person like that possibly know about loving someone else, Sam? — and how could I expect that you'd cause me any less pain than you caused your wives or your kids? — and I just wouldn't be able to take it so please leave me alone. It's okay. We had sex. We had a one night stand. You should go....Really. If you want to wash up or whatever you can. I'll gather your stuff —

SAM. No I won't go.

BRENDA. If you don't have money for a cab I can —

SAM. I can't go.

BRENDA. Don't make this any harder —

SAM. You don't want me to go.

BRENDA. I've asked you nicely.

SAM. Who do you think is coming for you when I walk out?

BRENDA. Go!

SAM. As flawed as I am, I'm here.

BRENDA. Go! JUST GO! GO! GET OUT, SAM! GO!
SAM. WHY! WHY! WHAT THE FUCK DO I HAVE
TO DO? WHY CAN'T YOU SEE? WHY CAN'T YOU SEE
THAT ALL I WANT TO DO IS GIVE YOU MY HEART?

*(SAM breaks down and cries. He slumps down to the ground
BRENDA looks at him and she starts to cry. She sits on the
ground next to him.)*

SAM. What the fuck are you crying about?

*(BRENDA is beside herself. She can't manage any words.
Beat.)*

SAM. *(Speaks the words.)*
I told him I didn't love him,
I watched as he confessed,
He was an actor really a waiter,
I stared up unimpressed.

I told him I didn't love him,
Told him several times,
Said the pock marks on his face were,
The penance for his crimes.

BRENDA. Pathetic.
SAM. You wrote that.
BRENDA. I know.
SAM. It's my other favorite song.
SAM. I told him I didn't love him, He said "hate me just
the same", he gently touched my shoulder, and sent my heart
a flame.

BRENDA. Doesn't even have a hook.

SAM. Sort of does.

SAM.
I said I didn't love him,
He turned handsome by the day,
choking on my loathing,
got on my knees to pray.

BRENDA. It'll never be a single.

SAM.
I said I didn't love him,
Climbing out the hole,
Sinning like a thief in the night,
Trying to steal a soul.

(Beat.)

SAM. That's what's different.

BRENDA. What's what's different?

SAM. You asked before why my marriages failed, right?

BRENDA. Yeah.

SAM. People make contracts with each other, do you agree?

BRENDA. What do you mean?

SAM. Said or unsaid, in marriages people accept the fact in this relationship work comes first or kids come first or whatever, you make sort of a deal with each other. It's not like you sign on the dotted line but people know what they're getting themselves into, right?

BRENDA. I guess.

SAM. My deal was I'm a musician. I'm a vagabond. I'm gonna be on the road, there's gonna be chicks around, there's gonna be drugs and I'm gonna be no better or no worse than anybody else. I'm not bringing anybody home. What happens on the road stays on the road...This was exciting to my first two wives for a while. They knew who the fuck I was, okay. We had kids and they wanted to change the deal and I wasn't able to... You want me to go?

BRENDA. What's different?

SAM. Our deal would be different.

BRENDA. How?

SAM. Well our contract now says we create together but we don't sleep together. That's already starting different for me.

BRENDA. We broke that contract.

SAM. I know.

BRENDA. What's our new contract?

SAM. I'm not sure. We're still writing it.

(BRENDA gets a pen and paper.)

BRENDA. So start the negotiations.

SAM. What negotiations?

BRENDA. What kind of contract could we make?

SAM. What do you want?

BRENDA. I'm not telling you what I want.

SAM. Why?

BRENDA. I don't negotiate like that.

SAM. Please, let's just put it all out on the table. What do you want?

BRENDA. I want you to get on your knees and propose marriage and give me a big fat ring.

SAM. Shut up.

BRENDA. Okay.

SAM. Are you serious?

BRENDA. Yes.

SAM. Do you love me?

BRENDA. I only sleep with guys I love, Sam.

SAM. So you've been waiting for this?

BRENDA. That has nothing to do with the deal.

SAM. So you want a guarantee?

BRENDA. Yes.

SAM. Do you know who you're talking to?

BRENDA. Yes.

SAM. I said til death do us apart twice and meant it both times and I left anyway.

BRENDA. I know.

BRENDA. I've never been married, Sam.

SAM. I know.

BRENDA. I've always wanted somebody to propose to me.

SAM. No one's ever proposed?

BRENDA. Not since I was nineteen and that was only cause he thought I was pregnant.

SAM. There is something pretty incredible about it.

BRENDA. What part?

SAM. The whole production. Making a big deal. Professing your love in front of your friends and family and God.

BRENDA. I want that, Sam!

SAM. Yeah?

BRENDA. What if the third time's the charm? What if all your other tremendous failures were supposed to lead you to this point?

SAM. I didn't say anything about tremendous failures.

BRENDA. Let's go with the spirit of the statement.

SAM. I can't marry you.

BRENDA. I knew it.

SAM. Knew what?

BRENDA. That you were a jerk.

SAM. I can't marry anybody. I'm not totally, officially divorced yet.

BRENDA. Oh my god!

SAM. I will be soon.

BRENDA. When?

SAM. I think it's another three months or maybe six. It's a promise I can't keep and I'm not in the habit of making those kinds of promises anymore.

BRENDA. So you're never getting married again?

SAM. Okay, I won't say never. I will say it's not something I'm willing to negotiate at this moment so if that's a deal breaker for you...I'm sorry.

(Beat.)

BRENDA. What sort of negotiation promises would you be willing to make?

SAM. About a relationship?

BRENDA. About a relationship with me.

SAM. ...I wouldn't go on the road without you...And I've never promised that to anyone.

BRENDA. Why would you promise it to me?

SAM. I wouldn't wanna be without you...

(BRENDA writes this down.)

BRENDA. What else?
SAM. I'd be a one woman guy and I'll stay sober.

(She continues to write.)

BRENDA. What else?...Would you be responsible?
SAM. How?
BRENDA. Like calling and showing up and being on time
—
SAM. I'm not that great at that.
BRENDA. What else aren't you great at?
SAM. ...Maybe you're right about me...With what you said.
BRENDA. What part of what I said?
SAM. ......Maybe at my core I don't love myself......Maybe I need help with that.

(BRENDA writes that down. She then puts down her pen. She stares at SAM for a long time.)

BRENDA. What else?
SAM. If we're together it won't be because I'm obligated to you by law. It won't be because it's the right thing to do. It won't be because I promised my mother. It won't be because you're pregnant. It won't be because I feel sorry for you. It will be because I can't bear the thought of being without you.
BRENDA. What else?
SAM. I'll do my part. I'll work at it. I'll clean my side of the street. I'm ready for this. I'm so ready...Can't you see that?
BRENDA. I can see that.
SAM. Yeah?

BRENDA. I saw it in your eyes when you came in the door.

SAM. You did?

BRENDA. You looked different.

SAM. In what way.

BRENDA. You were all full up...All full up with life.

SAM. Yeah?

BRENDA. And I wanted that too.

SAM. ...So what would you be willing to do?

BRENDA. I would do laundry.

SAM. Laundry?

BRENDA. I actually like doing laundry and I like washing dishes. It relaxes me but don't take advantage, okay?

SAM. Okay.

BRENDA. And I'm a really good cook and I like cooking for people.

SAM. Okay...How are you with money?

BRENDA. Not great but not horrible.

SAM. Are you in debt?

BRENDA. No.

SAM. I am...For child support.

BRENDA. I'm not fixing that.

SAM. I don't expect you to.

BRENDA. I'm crazy, Sam.

SAM. I know.

BRENDA. It's real.

SAM. How so?

(Beat.)

BRENDA. I sometimes get depressed and I'm paranoid and I'm anxious and I listen to the wrong voices sometimes.

SAM. That scares me.

BRENDA. It scares me too.

SAM. I really hate that part. I really do. I mean, you get nasty and I don't know if I can stomach it.

BRENDA. You gotta take the good with the bad right?

SAM. Talk to me about the good.

(BRENDA holds the sheet up and is about to tear it.)

BRENDA. I'll love you all up, Sam and I'll make you laugh and we'll make music together and I'll be good to your children because I'm a big kid and you'll never be bored and I'm a very loyal person, I promise you that.

SAM. Can we do a song?

BRENDA. Do you want to sign this thing?

SAM. Maybe...Can we do a song?

BRENDA. What's that?

SAM. The remix.

BRENDA. You're not gonna give up til you get your way.

SAM. The Remix

BRENDA. What do you think about what I just said?...I thought it was pretty, ya know, important, Sam.

SAM. Listen.

SAM.

(Sings)

I SEE THE STRENGTH YOU HIDE

I'VE WATCHED YOU LAUGH AND PLAY

I FEEL YOU UNDERSTAND

YOUR EYES ARE WONDERFUL

YOU MAKE ME LIGHT INSIDE

YOU HAVE A WAY THAT PULLS

EVERYTHINGS TURNING INTO BEAUTIFUL
COME AND BE MY GIRL
COME AND FILL MY WORLD
COME AND MAKE ME SMILE COME AND STAY INSIDE
    MY LIFE

    (He raps)
COME STAY WITH ME FOR MORE THAN A MINUTE
I FEEL I STARTED SOMETHING THAT I'VE GOTTA
    FINISH
COME TAKE A WALK WITH ME THROUGH
    BROOKLYN,
TALK WITH ME, SMOKE A NEWPORT IN NEW YORK
    WITH ME
COME SPEND A NIGHT WITH YOUR MAN IN TRIBECA
WATCH A FLICK FROM JAPAN ON A PROJECTOR

FORGET YOU EVER HAD A LOVE IN YOUR LIFE
THEY WEREN'T LOVING YOUR RIGHT YOU WEREN'T
HUSBAND AND WIFE
COME HUG ME TONIGHT MAKE LOVE IN THE LIGHT
I KNOW I'M RUBBING YOU RIGHT CAUSE YOU FEEL
    THE SAME
WAY THAT I DO
WHEN I HEAR YOUR NAME GET ON THE TRAIN ITS
TIME TO GET THIS STARTED

TAKE THE 9 UPTOWN TO GET OFF AT MY APARTMENT
SIT ON THE CARPET,
I'LL SET THE MOOD FOR YOU
EVERYTHINGS TURNING INTO BEAUTIFUL.....

SAM. Sing this. *He hands her the new words.*

BRENDA.
I FEEL YOUR SHINE ON ME
I TASTE YOUR LAUGHTER TOO
I SEE THE SUN IN YOU
YOU MAKE ME FEEL SO FULL
YOU TURN MY LIFE AROUND
YOUR HEART MEANS EVERYTHING AND
EVERYTHINGS TURNING INTO BEAUTIFUL
COME AND BE MY MAN
COME AND TAKE MY HAND
COME AND MAKE ME SMILE COME AND STAY INSIDE
    MY LIFE.

*(SAM carries her back to the bed. They kiss. Lights start to
    dim.)*

BRENDA. What did you mean when you said the real
fear?

SAM. The real fear?

BRENDA. Before you said the real fear. Something like
the outside drama did something and then I was protecting
myself from the real fear.

SAM. I don't know what I meant.

BRENDA. C'mon Sam.

SAM. Sometimes I just say things...They sound good...
What do you think the real fear is?

BRENDA. Getting older...Letting go of all those rock n
roll fantasies.

SAM. I'm not your fantasy guy?
BRENDA. I sure hope not...

(Lights out.)

PROPERTY PLOT

Act One

Knitting, leg warmers, 2 needles, yarn
Glass of wine x2, 1 a quarter full
Guitar w/ strap, capo on 5th fret
Bottle of water
Mic with stand
Guitar in soft case
Capo
Egg
Mug of tea
CD
Lyric sheet
Video camera

Act Two

Guitar
Bottle of water
Pen
Journal

COSTUME PLOT

Brenda

Bras
Underwear
Henley shirt
Long johns
Cardigan
Slippers (silver Burks, something with spark)
Velvet coat (something softly textured)
Top hat/crazy hat
Spiky heels
Sunglasses
Slip
Jeans
Tattoos

Sam

Vintage leather jacket
Hoodie
Jeans
Motorcycle boots
Boxers
Hat
Socks
T-Shirt
Tattoos